Disney's
A Picnic in the Woods

Random House 🏠 New York

Ⓖ GROLIER
BOOK CLUB EDITION

ISBN: 0–394–85873–5
123   K L M

It's a beautiful day for a picnic!
Mickey drives Minnie and his nephews
to a park in the woods.
Everyone helps unpack the car.
"When do we eat?" ask the boys.

"Let's play baseball first," says Mickey. "Batter up!"

He pitches a fast ball to Minnie.

CRACK!
Minnie slams the ball!

It's a home run!
The ball sails into the bushes.
The boys run to find it.
"It must be in here somewhere," says Morty.
"Watch out! Don't touch!" says Ferdie. "That's poison ivy!"
The ball game is over.

Suddenly it begins to rain.
"Quick! Into the shelter!" cries Minnie.
Mickey grabs the picnic basket and runs.

"We can have our picnic right in here,"
says Mickey. "I'll light the charcoal now."

Soon the coals are ready.
Mickey and the boys roast the hot dogs.

"I bet I can eat
three hot dogs,"
says Ferdie.

Hot dogs and lemonade—what a treat!
"Who cares about the rain?" says
Minnie. "This is fun!"

The rain stops
by the end of lunch.
"Let's take a walk,"
says Mickey.
Off they all go.

In the open picnic area
they see:

a bumblebee

a robin feeding
its babies

red clover

dandelions

a robin
catching
a worm

a squirrel

They come to a stream in the woods.
"Hold my hand," says Mickey.
He helps Minnie cross the stream.
The boys build a dam with rocks.
They are too busy to see the turtle.

Here are some animals and plants
that live along the stream:

red salamander

painted turtle

snail

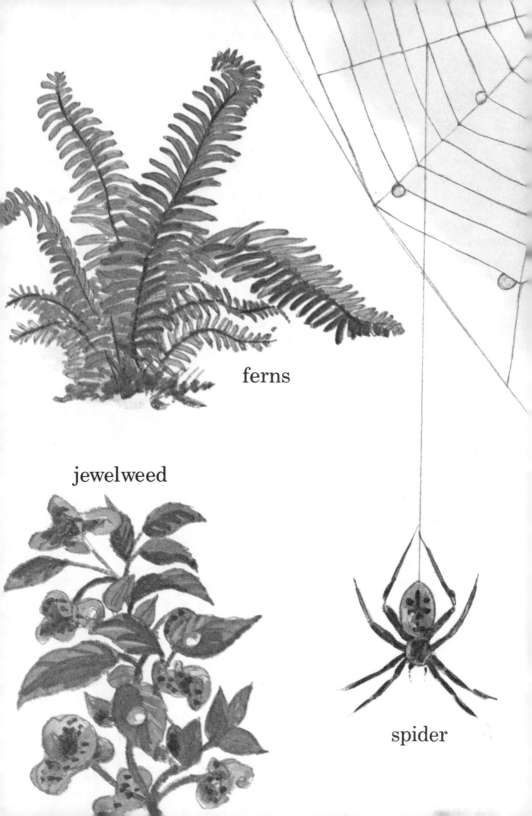

ferns

jewelweed

spider

Deep in the woods it is dark and cool.
Some birds are looking for bugs in
tree bark.

Chipmunks look for nuts and seeds.

Lots of mushrooms grow here, but not
many flowers.

They come to a clearing in the woods.
They see some ripe blackberries.
"Careful when you pick them," says Mickey
to the boys. "Watch out for the prickles."

Butterflies flit from flower
to flower.
Minnie snaps their pictures.

Animals come into the clearing to eat.
Many flowers and grasses grow there.

rabbit

Queen Anne's lace

honeybees in
red clover

monarch butterfly

black-eyed Susan

milkweed

deer

They find a pond in the woods.
Ducks are swimming on it.
Water lilies grow in the shallow water.
"I'm going to catch a frog," says Ferdie.
But the frogs are too fast for him!

Late in the day mosquitoes
suddenly appear.

There are hundreds of them!
They all try to bite Mickey
and Minnie and the boys.

"Here," says Minnie. "Put on
some insect repellant. And then
I think it's time to go home."

They hate to leave the woods.
But the beautiful day is over.